For Sabine

and a big hug for Monika,
who likes to read all the
funny voices, not not necessarily
in the right order.

D.M.

TITLE:

THE GHOST LIBRARY

AUTHOR:

by David Melling

First edition for the United States and Canada published in
2004 by Barron's Educational Series, Inc.
Published in arrangement with Hodder Children's Books

First publised in Great Britain in 2004 by Hodder Children's Books, a
division of Hodder Headline Limited, 338 Euston Road, London NW1 3BH

Copyright © David Melling 2004
The author and illustrator asserts the moral right to be identified
as the author and illustrator of this work.

All inquiries should be addressed to:
Barron's Educational Series, Inc.
250 Wireless Boulevard
Hauppauge, New York 11788
http://www.barronseduc.com

International Standard Book No.: 0-7641-5791-4

Library of Congress Catalog Card No.: 2004090459

Printed in China
9 8 7 6 5 4 3 2 1

**IF YOU DON'T RETURN THIS BOOK TO
THE GHOST LIBRARY WE'RE COMING TO GET IT!**

THE GHOST LIBRARY

DAVID MELLING

BARRON'S

Bo had gone to bed early. She wasn't tired so she decided to read her favorite book. The story was great—it was about a witch who had smelly feet.

And Bo had just got to the interesting part about strawberry-flavored socks, when without warning...

...the lights went out!

Bo felt a cold chill.

Whispers sniffled
and snuffled in
the dark.

"I can't see a thing!"

"It's here somewhere!"

"Ow,
that's my
nose!"

Shadows
shivered
closer.

A clammy hand grabbed BO'S book.

It was so sudden and Bo was holding it so tightly

that the book and Bo were jerked into the air!

"GOT IT!" squealed a voice!

Bo kept her eyes shut and tried not to let go.

So she didn't see how she passed through her
bedroom wall, into the night sky, and toward
a very tall tower that hadn't been there five minutes ago!

Before she knew it, Bo found herself in...

"I must be dreaming," thought Bo. She had never met any ghosts before, but she had always imagined that if she ever did, they would look very different to the three smiling at her now!

"Errr, hello," said the tall one. "I'm Magpie."

"I'm Twit," said another, floating around her head.

"And I'm Puddle Mud," said a third voice from somewhere near her slippers. "What a surprise. Welcome to The Ghost Library."

"What do you mean 'surprise'?" said Bo.
"You brought me here."

"Um, yes," said Magpie, looking a little uncomfortable.
"The thing is, we wanted your book, but you wouldn't
let go. So you...*came* with it." He gave the book in Bo's
hand another little tug.

"We collect books for our library," said Twit.

Bo looked up at the shelves. "But it's completely empty!"

"You tried to steal my book," said Bo crossly.

"Oh no," spluttered Puddle Mud. "We're not thieves. Only we don't have our own books, so we take children's books, read them a few times, then . . . we give them back!"

They looked sad and Magpie honked noisily into a tissue.

"Let's have a story," said Twit quickly. They all looked at Bo.

"You want me to read you a story?" she said.

"Well, now that you're here, that would be lovely!" they said.

"STORY TIME!" yelped Twit.

All at once, Bo felt a terrible draft, as ghost after ghost flew into the library and popped out of the shelves.

As soon as they saw her, the ghosts started chattering excitedly.

"Goodness, who's that?"

"I don't know, but I hope it's a good story!"

Eventually, the murmuring stopped and it became very quiet. They waited.

Bo sighed. She sat down and began to read her book about the witch.

"In a dark and gloomy cave lived a witch, whose terrible feet were so stinky that her cat wore a clothes pin on its nose.
This made it very difficult to purr . . ."

". . . and so, as long as she kept her boots on forever, she never smelled her feet again!" Bo closed the book.

The ghosts were spellbound.

"Wow, that was a great story!" they said. Tell us another."

"No," said Bo. "Now it's your turn. Why don't you tell me a story."

"Oh, we couldn't possibly," they blushed.

"We don't know any," said Magpie.

"That's why we borrow books. We're the Story Book Collectors."

"But you can make up any story you like. Just look around you—they're everywhere!" said Bo.

Twit looked in his pockets. Then he took a peek in Puddle Mud's. Then they all started looking.

"No, not like that," laughed Bo. "I'll help you. Let's swap ideas."

The ghosts were so excited they all shouted their ideas at once.

"There must be ghosts in it that make loud jibbery noises!"

"And sneaky creepy shadows!"

"With squinty eyes and spider-breath!"

"Of course!" cried Bo. "Let's tell
A GHOST STORY!"

The ghosts decided that Bo was the best at
reading stories because she put funny voices in
in all the right places. So they settled down and
listened to her read their story:

"One damp and spooky night, three Story Book Collectors crept
into the bedroom of a little girl called Bo . . ."

... and to this day The Ghost Library is full of stories.

They're mostly about ghosts but, if you look
hard enough, you can find one about a witch,
a cat, and a clothes pin.

When Bo returned to her room she found a small card on her pillow.

On it were little silver letters that danced and glowed as she read...

FRIENDS OF THE GHOST LIBRARY
FULL MEMBERSHIP

And now, sometimes Bo visits The Ghost Library, and sometimes the ghosts visit her!

Whichever it is, they always insist that she reads to them... with all the funny voices in all the right places!